Are You A Monkey?

A TALE OF
ANIMAL CHARADES

Marine Rivoal

English text freely adapted by Maria Tunney
from the original text by Marine Rivoal

φ

High up in the trees, the birds
were excitedly chitchatting.
Down on the ground, the animals
were curious about all the fuss.

Little Starfish was curious too!
He climbed up onto his rock,
eager to see what was going on.

Parrot fluffed up her feathers and
spread her wings wide.
"Guess who I am!" she said.
"You're a . . . pineapple?" ventured Toucan.
"No, silly! I'm a LION!" laughed Parrot.
"Look! Down there!" interrupted Cockatoo.
He'd spotted someone below.

Crocodile called up to the birds.
"What are you doing? It sounds like fun!"
"We're playing charades!" said Cockatoo.
"You just think of an animal or a thing, act it out . . .
and then we guess what you are!
Do you want to try?"

Crocodile jumped into position! "Can you guess who I am?"

"You're something long . . ." said Cockatoo.
". . . that sticks out of the ground," said Parrot.
"I know! You're a CARROT!" exclaimed Toucan.

"He's not a carrot — he's an ostrich, like ME!"
said Ostrich, joining in the fun.
"I stick my head into the ground to check on my eggs.
The sand makes a perfect, snug nest."

"Well played, Crocodile!" said Toucan.
"Who wants to try next?"

"I have a charade!" said Ostrich,
and she arched her neck back.
"Can you guess who I am?"

"You're something bendy . . ."
said Cockatoo.
"And something *watery* . . ."
said Parrot.
"Are you . . . a CUCUMBER?"
guessed Toucan.

"A cucumber? No, she's an elephant like me!
I suck water up into my trunk and
spray it on my back to cool down."

"This is getting exciting!"
said Toucan, hopping from
one foot to the other.
"Who wants to play now?"

"Me! I want to play!" said Elephant.
"Alley-oop! Up, up I GO!
Can you guess who I am?"

"You're something that hangs from a tree . . ." said Cockatoo.
"Are you a bat?" asked Parrot.
"YOU'RE A BANANA!" yelled Toucan.
(He was *sure* this time.)

"No, not a bat OR a banana — she's a monkey like me! I swing by my tail, like this, so my hands are free to grab some fruit for lunch."

"Excellent charade, Elephant!" said Toucan. "Now let's see what *you* can do, Monkey!"

Monkey climbed up into the tree
and curled into position.
"Can you guess who I am?" he said.

"You're something that hugs
a branch . . ." said Cockatoo.
   "A caterpillar!" said Parrot.
      "A COCONUT!" said Toucan.

"No, not a caterpillar OR a coconut,
he's a chameleon, like me!
When I hide, I hold very, very still.
My skin changes shades,
so that I look like a leaf on the branch!"

Toucan could barely see Chameleon . . .
He really was good at hiding.

"My turn!" said Chameleon.
"Can you guess who I am?"

"You're something long and wriggly . . ." said Cockatoo.
"A worm?" said Parrot.
"Our dessert!" giggled Toucan.
(He was getting VERY hungry!)

"No, NOT your dessssssert!
He's a snake like me!
With my long body,
I slither my way around —
looking for *my* dessert!"

Toucan hopped out of Snake's reach.
He didn't want to be *anyone's* dessert!

Snake coiled and curled her long body
into a most curious shape . . .

"Now, birds," she said.
"See if you can guess this charade . . ."

Parrot tilted her head.
Cockatoo scratched his beak.
But they couldn't guess.
Even Toucan didn't have a clue!

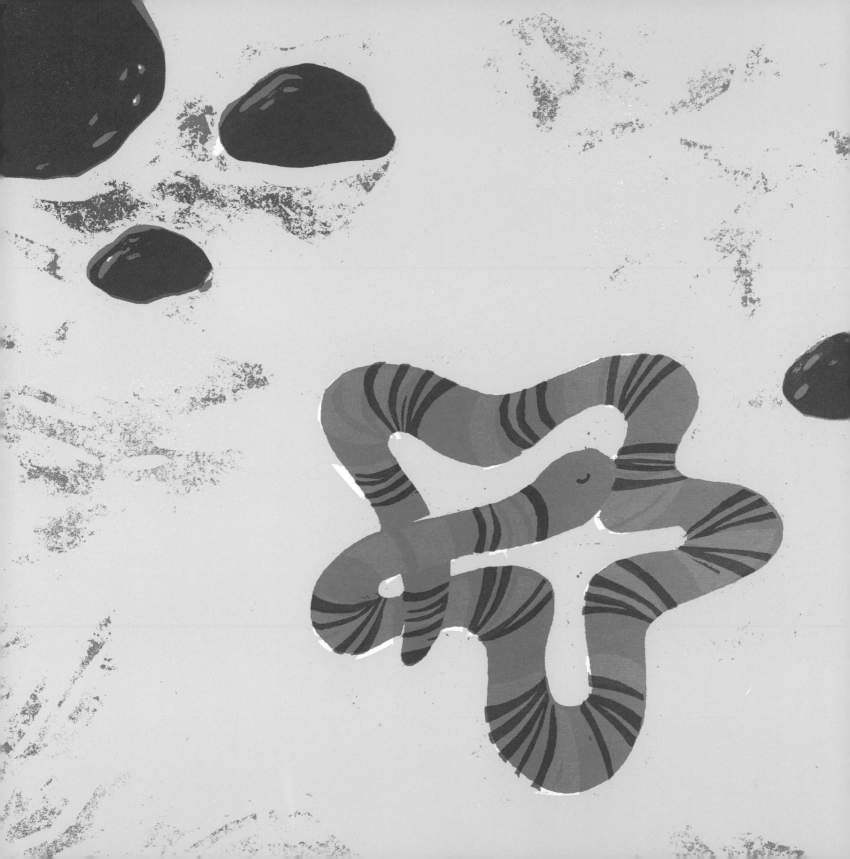

"You're me!" said a tiny voice from the water.
"You're right, Little Starfish, it *is* you!" said Snake.
"Now, show us what you can do!"

"I *wish* I could play," said Little Starfish, sighing.
"But I can't jump, or hang, or change my shape.
I can't do . . . anything."

The animals fell silent —
what could Little Starfish be?

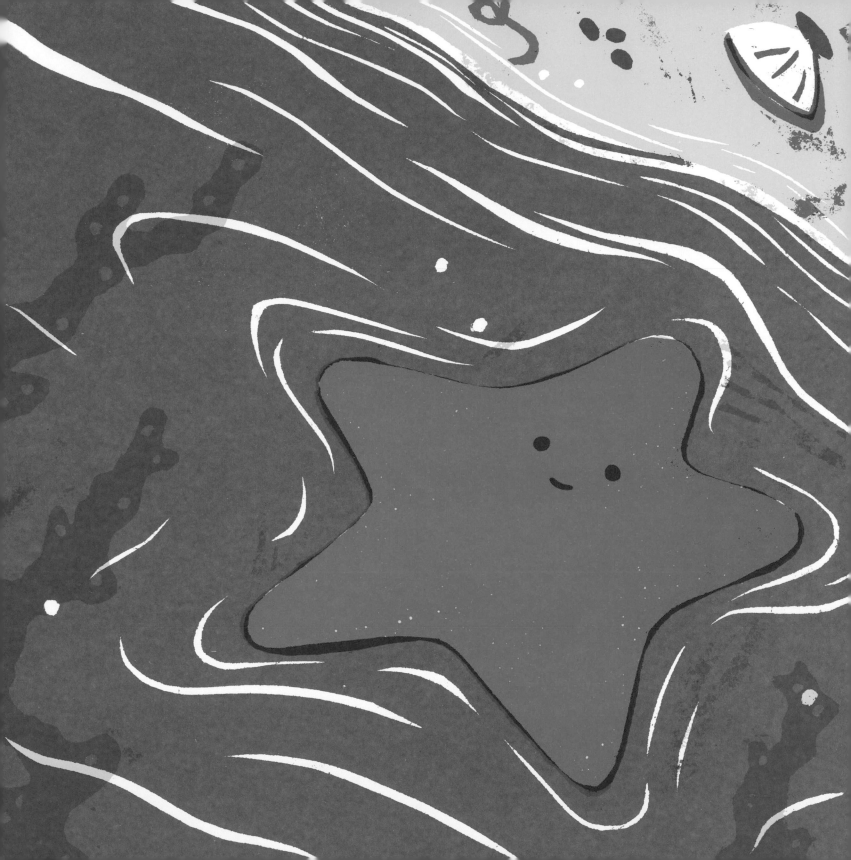

Elephant had an idea!
She gently scooped up Little Starfish
and sprayed him high up into the air.

"A SHOOTING STAR!" Toucan cooed.

"You got it!" cried Elephant. "You guessed *right*!"
Everyone cheered, chirped, and roared!

And all the animals agreed that Little Starfish's charade
was the very best one of all.